TELLING THE TRUTH

A Book about Lying

CAROLYN LARSEN
ILLUSTRATED BY TIM O'CONNOR

BakerBooks

a division of Baker Publishing Group
Grand Rapids, Michigan

Text © 2016 by Carolyn Larsen
Illustrations © 2016 by Baker Publishing Group

Published by Baker Books
a division of Baker Publishing Group
P.O. Box 6287, Grand Rapids, MI 49516-6287
www.bakerbooks.com

Printed in the United States of America

Library of Congress Cataloging-in-Publication Data
Names: Larsen, Carolyn, 1950– author.
Title: Telling the truth : a book about lying / Carolyn Larsen ;
    illustrated by Tim O'Connor.
Description: Grand Rapids : Baker Books, 2016. | Series:
    Growing God's kids
Identifiers: LCCN 2016011306 | ISBN 9780801009266
Subjects: LCSH: Truthfulness and falsehood—Religious
    aspects—Christianity—Juvenile literature. | Truthfulness
    and falsehood in children—Juvenile literature. | Bible.
    Colossians, III, 9—Criticism, interpretation, etc.—Juvenile
    literature.
Classification: LCC BV4647.T7 L37 2016 | DDC 241/.3—
    dc23
LC record available at https://lccn.loc.gov/2016011306

Scripture quotation is from the Contemporary English Version © 1991, 1992, 1995 by American Bible Society. Used by permission.

19 20 21 22   7 6 5 4

Stop lying to each other.
You have given up your old
way of life with its habits.

COLOSSIANS 3:9

See that boy? That's Max.
Sometimes he says things he
knows aren't true. That's called lying,
and Max does it on purpose!

My name is Leonard, and
I'm Max's favorite toy.

Max's mom has a rule: Play soccer outside—not in the house. "Things get broken when balls are kicked inside," she tells Max.

Even though Max knows the rule, he kicks his soccer ball into the living room. Crash! Bang! It hits a lamp and breaks it.

"I didn't do it!" Max says.

Mom knows that Max is not telling the truth. He is telling a lie.

"It's important to always tell the truth, even if you're afraid to tell me," Mom reminds Max.

Sometimes it is scary to admit when we have done something wrong. But the problem is that Max lies when he knows he has disobeyed. He lies to avoid being punished.

"Lying about what you have done will just get you into more trouble," Mom tells Max. "You should always tell the truth, even if you have disobeyed the rules."

- He should just tell Mom what happened.
- He should tell her that he is sorry for disobeying.
- He should tell her that he will try not to lie again.

Stop lying to each other.
Colossians 3:9

11

Max likes to play with his friends on the playground. But Alex is one boy Max doesn't like. That's because Alex is sometimes mean to Max.

Max wants to get Alex in trouble. He sees a chance to do that when a little boy gets hurt.

Max tells his teacher, Mrs. Roberts, that Alex pushed the little boy down.

Max is lying. Alex did not hurt the little boy. The other kids saw what happened and tell the teacher the truth.

Mrs. Roberts asks Max if he lied about Alex. He admits that he did. "You must apologize to Alex," Mrs. Roberts says. "Instead of trying to get him in trouble, you should tell a grown-up when he is mean to you."

"I'm sorry, Alex," Max says. "Want to play soccer with me?"

Stop lying to each other.
Colossians 3:9

17

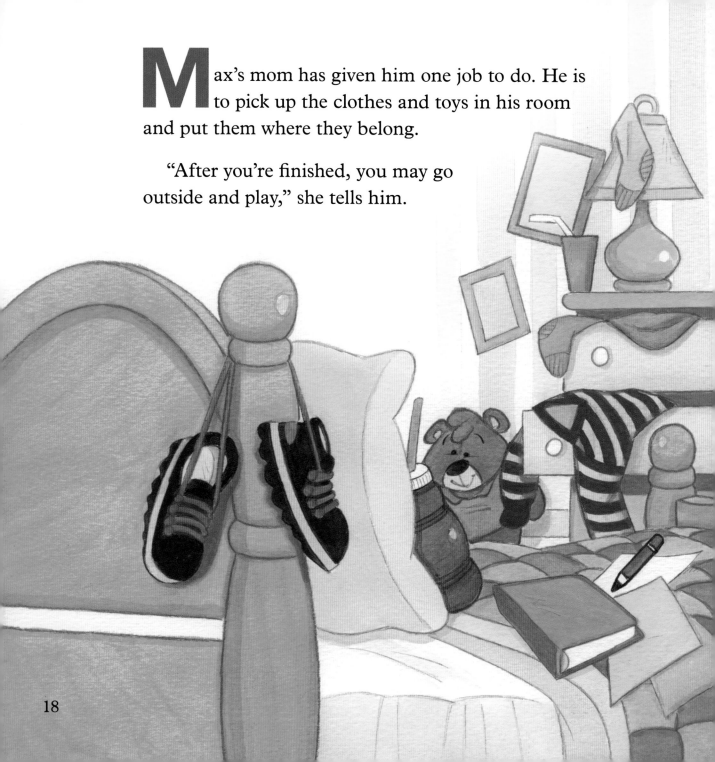

Max's mom has given him one job to do. He is to pick up the clothes and toys in his room and put them where they belong.

"After you're finished, you may go outside and play," she tells him.

18

"I'm finished with my room, Mom. I'm going outside now," Max calls.

"Hold on, partner," Mom says as she goes to check his room. "Did you put your things where they belong?"

"Yep, I did," Max says.

Mom knows he isn't telling the truth. She can see the books and clothes under his bed.

Mom tells Max, "You were told to put things away where they belong. Because you didn't and lied about it, you won't be able to play outside."

Max learns that he should have done his chore right the first time. He tells his mom he's sorry he lied. She's happy when Max puts his things where they belong.

Stop lying to each other.
Colossians 3:9

Max loves candy. Chocolate is his favorite.

Mom gives him two candy bars and tells him one is for his brother, Zach.

But Max eats both of them himself! Zach runs to tell Mom.

"Why didn't you give your brother his candy?" Mom asks Max.

"I did!" Max lies. "I gave it to him and he ate it!"

Mom sees the chocolate on Max's face and finds two candy wrappers on the floor. She knows Max is lying.

Mom is very sad that Max has lied to her.

Mom tells Max she knows that chocolate candy is his favorite. She reminds him that telling the truth is important.

"I'm going to punish you for lying about giving a candy bar to your brother," Mom says. "No chocolate for a week, Max."

Max is sorry that he lied, and he's sad he won't get to have chocolate for seven whole days.

Stop lying to each other.
Colossians 3:9

 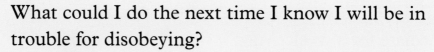
What could I do the next time I know I will be in trouble for disobeying?

1. Tell my parents what happened.
2. Tell my parents the truth when they ask.

What can I do when I want to get someone in trouble by lying about them?

1. Tell a grown-up what the other person did.
2. Tell the other person I don't like how they are treating me.
3. Think about how my lie hurts others.

What should I do when I want to lie instead of doing my job?

1. Just do the job anyway.
2. Make doing the job a game so it's more fun.
3. Understand that doing jobs will help me learn to become more grown-up.

Instead of lying when I don't want to share, I could . . .

1. Think about what the punishment for my lies might be.
2. Think about how the person would feel if they didn't get what they were supposed to.
3. Share without complaining, because learning to share will help me in all of my life.

Remember

God says not to lie because that shows disrespect to others. (See Ephesians 4:25.)

God says that he dislikes lying more than almost anything else. (See Proverbs 6:16–17.)

God says honesty is the best . . . always. (See Proverbs 12:22.)

God says to tell the truth so others will respect and trust you. (See Colossians 3:9.)

When someone lies to you, you find it hard to trust them again. It's scary to know you are going to be punished or that you have disappointed someone by your behavior, but lying is never OK. Lying just causes a bigger problem.

Stop lying to each other.
Colossians 3:9